S0-DVC-174

the Hedgehog

The Golden Goose

Rumpelstiltskin

Snow White and Rose Red

The Musicians of Bremen

This title was originally cataloged by the Library of Congress as follows:
Grimm, Jakob Ludwig Karl, 1785–1863.
Grimm's fairy tales, retold by Rose Dobbs. Illustrated by Gertrude Elliott
Espenscheid. Prepared under the supervision of Josette Frank. New York,
Random House, ᶜ1955. unpaged. illus. 29 cm.
1. Fairy tales. ɪ. Grimm, Wilhelm Karl, 1786–1859, joint author. ɪɪ. Dobbs,
Rose. PZ8.G882F 67 55–6063 ‡
ISBN: 0-394-80657-3   ISBN: 0-394-90657-8 (lib. ed.)

.

Grimm's Fairy Tales

Retold by **Rose Dobbs**

Illustrated by

Gertrude Elliott Espenscheid

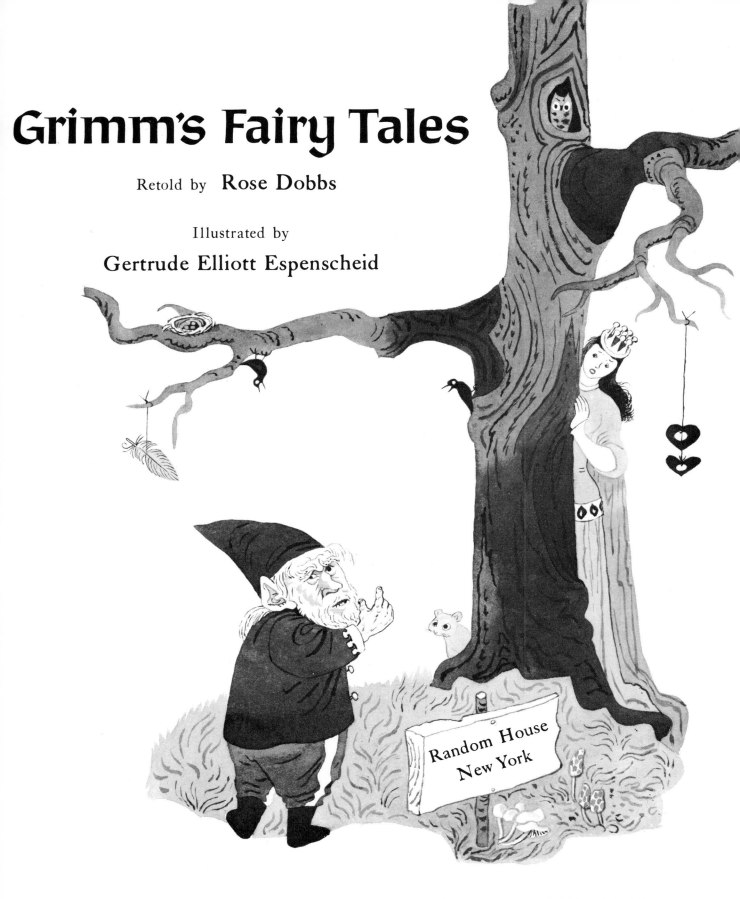

Random House
New York

Prepared under the supervision of JOSETTE FRANK, Children's Book Adviser of the Child Study Association of America. Copyright 1955 by Random House, Inc. All rights reserved under International and Pan-American Copyright Conventions. Published in New York by Random House, Inc. and simultaneously in Toronto, Canada by Random House of Canada Limited. Manufactured in the U.S.A.

The Brave Little Tailor

Once upon a time a merry little tailor fixed himself a snack of bread and jam, put it down for a moment, and returned to the suit he was stitching. Before he knew it, a host of flies, attracted by the fragrance of the jam, huzzed and buzzed around him and settled down on the bread.

"Hey!" cried the tailor. "What's this? I don't remember inviting any of you. Shoo! Away! Swoosh!"

But the flies did not understand English. So they paid no attention at all; only settled more thickly on the bread.

"I'll soon fix that," said the tailor. He took a length of cloth and went after the flies, swishing smartly right and left. The flies scattered like dust in a windstorm—except those that were slain.

When the air cleared, the little tailor counted the dead flies.

One   two   three   four   five   six   seven!

"Seven!" he cried. "Seven at one blow! What a brave fellow I am! The whole town must hear of this!"

In a twinkling he cut out and sewed up a vest on which he stitched in large white letters: *SEVEN AT ONE BLOW*.

He put on the vest and paused to admire himself. As he stood thus before his mirror, a thought came to him. "The town, did I say? No, the whole world must hear of this. Seven at one blow! Was there ever such a remarkable deed?"

No sooner said than done. The brave little tailor put a cheese (to sustain him in his travels) in one pocket, and his pet bird (to keep him company) in the other pocket. He set his cap at a jaunty angle on his head, closed his shop, and started off in search of adventure and fortune.

After traveling for some time, he came to a hill on top of which sat an ugly, fierce giant, surveying the world. The little tailor went up to the giant and called out boldly:

"Hi, my friend! What's the point of just sitting here? Why not join me? I'm off to make my fortune. We should make good traveling companions!"

The giant looked down at the tailor scornfully. "Why, you miserable rascal," he said, "you runt, you puny little man, you——"

"Softly, softly," said the tailor. "Size doesn't make a man, but deeds do. Before you say another word, take a look at this." And he opened his jacket and showed the giant his vest.

"Seven at one blow!" read the giant in astonishment, never dreaming that it was seven flies, not men, that the tailor had slain. He now regarded him with some respect. "Is it possible," he said to himself, "that this creature who is so small I can hardly see him has actually slain seven at one blow?" And to the tailor he said, "Let's see if you are as strong as you claim."

He picked up a stone and squeezed it so hard that water ran out of it. The little tailor was not daunted. He put his hand in his pocket, took out the cheese and squeezed it so hard that the whey ran out of it.

The giant's eyes almost popped out of his head. "That wasn't much of a trick," he said, "but how about this?" He picked up another stone and threw it up so high in the air that many minutes went by before the stone returned, dripping wet. "See," said the giant, "that stone reached the highest cloud in the sky."

"Not a bad throw," said the tailor, "but when *I* throw something up in the air, it *never* comes back." And he took the bird out of his other pocket and threw it up into the air. The bird, happy to be set free, spread its wings and was soon out of sight. They waited and waited but the bird did not come back.

Now the giant was truly frightened. He certainly did not want to travel with such a remarkable fellow. But he also did not want to risk offending him. So he said politely, "It would be a great pleasure to join you, but it so happens that I have pressing business to attend to." Without even waiting for the tailor's reply, the giant took to his heels. In a few moments all that could be seen of him was the cloud of dust he raised as he sped away.

The little tailor, laughing merrily, continued on his way. He traveled all day and at nightfall, feeling somewhat weary, came to a palace courtyard. Here he found a soft grassy spot and was soon fast asleep. As he lay there, several persons came by and, examining him from all sides, saw the vest with large white letters on it:

SEVEN AT ONE BLOW

"This must be a mighty warrior," they said to one another. "The King should be told. In case of war, a man like this could be worth a whole army." And off they went and told the King, who gave orders to have the stout warrior brought before him.

The tailor awoke to find himself the object of much attention. He was brought to the King who, marveling that so little a man could be so big a hero, invited him to enter his service.

"Nothing would suit me better," said the tailor.

So he was taken to the soldiers' barracks and treated with much respect. This made the other soldiers envious and they plotted to get rid of him. At last some of them went to the King.

"It is not fair, your Majesty," they said, "to expect us to get along with one who slays seven at a blow. Just suppose one of us should offend the fellow. Why, he could make an end of your whole army in no time!"

The King did not want to lose his men. He began to wish the tailor had never set foot in his courtyard. But how to get rid of him? At last an idea came to the King. Calling the tailor, he said:

"In my woods live two monstrous giants who are terrifying the countryside. If you can do away with them, I will give you the Princess, my only daughter, for your wife, and half my kingdom besides. If you can't, you must leave and never come back."

"A princess and half a kingdom aren't given away every day in the week," said the tailor. "Those giants are as good as dead."

But the King did not trust the little man and thought he was only boasting. So he sent a company of his best soldiers, on horseback, along with him. When they reached the woods, the tailor told the horsemen to wait there.

"He who slays seven at one blow doesn't need any help to get

rid of two," he said, and he entered the woods alone.

He had not ventured far when he heard roars and rumbles like thunder. Following the sounds he came upon the two giants, fast asleep. Their snores shook the very air. The little tailor picked up two heavy rocks and climbed up into a tree directly above the sleeping monsters. Then he dropped one of the rocks *plop!* right down on the chest of the first giant. The big fellow sat up and nudged his companion.

"Why did you throw this rock at me?" he asked angrily.

"You're dreaming," said the other, angry, too, at being awakened. "I didn't throw anything. Let me alone."

And they both went back to sleep. When he heard them snoring again, the little tailor dropped the other rock on the chest of the second giant. This one sat up with a start and poked the other sharply in the ribs.

"I told you to let me alone," he snarled furiously.

"I didn't touch you," shouted the first.

They began to argue. From arguing they went to quarreling and from quarreling to fighting. In their rage they tore up many of the surrounding trees. Each took the biggest tree and, using it as a club, went at the other and soon there was an end of both. When he saw the giants stretched out dead, the tailor climbed down from the tree and called the horsemen. They came at a gallop, expecting to find him torn to pieces, judging from all the commotion they had heard. But there he stood, as merry as ever, and at his feet lay the two terrible giants, cold and dead!

When the King heard this, he had no choice but to keep his promise. The little tailor married the Princess and got half the kingdom; and when the old King died, he got the other half.

And so you see how easily a tailor can become a King, if the tailor is both smart and brave.

The Musicians of Bremen

A FAITHFUL DONKEY had toiled long and hard for many years carrying heavy sacks of grain to the mill. At last, old and worn out, his strength failed, and he grew more and more unfit for work. Seeing this, his master thought: "That old donkey isn't earning his keep any longer." And he began to think how he might best get rid of him. The donkey felt in his bones that something unpleasant was being planned, so he ran away and took the road to Bremen. He had heard of a good street band there and thought he might join them and become town musician.

As he walked along, he came upon a big hunting dog lying in the road, panting as if he had just finished a race.

"Ho there," said the donkey, "why are you panting so, Old Gripper?"

"Alas," replied the dog, "just because I am now old and can no longer hunt with the pack, my master wanted to kill me. So I ran away. But what shall I do to earn my bread?"

"Why not join me?" asked the donkey. "I am on my way to Bremen to become town musician. I will play the lute, and you can beat the kettle-drum."

This sounded good to the dog, so he agreed, and the two traveled on together. Before long they met a cat. She was sitting in the middle of the road, wearing a face as long as a three-day rainy spell.

"Ho there, Whisker-trimmer," called the donkey. "What makes you look so cheerful?"

"How can one be cheerful," sighed the cat, "when one's life is in danger? Because I am now old and my teeth are not as sharp as they used to be, and I would rather purr before the fire than chase after mice, my mistress wanted to drown me. So I ran away. Well and good. But what am I to do now?"

"Why not join us?" asked the donkey. "We are on our way to Bremen to become town musicians. You have had so much practice in the art of night serenading, you should have no trouble at all finding a welcome in the band."

This idea appealed to the cat, so she went with them. A short while later, the three runaways came to a farmyard where a rooster sat upon the gate post crowing with all his might.

"Softly, softly, Red-comb," said the donkey. "Your shriek pierces one through bone and marrow. Why are you raising such a clatter?"

"I'm crowing while I can," said the rooster. "Even though I can still foretell good weather, the farmer's wife has other plans for me. She expects guests for Sunday dinner and has ordered the cook to make me into soup. My neck's to be wrung tonight, so while I still can be heard, I'm crowing with all my might."

"But that's such a waste of talent," said the donkey. "You had better come with us. We're on our way to Bremen to become town musicians. When all of us make music together, your voice will add just the right finishing touch to our concert."

The rooster allowed himself to be persuaded into joining them and all four traveled on together. But the town of Bremen was too far away to be reached in one day. By evening, the four friends came to a deep forest where they decided to spend the night. The donkey and the dog made themselves comfortable at the foot of a big tree. The cat and the rooster settled in the branches, the rooster choosing the highest where he felt most safe. Before going to sleep, he took a good look around in all directions. Suddenly he called down to his companions:

"I think I see a light in the distance. There must be a house not too far off."

"If that is so," said the donkey, "perhaps we should find out. A house would give us better shelter than this tree."

The dog agreed and thought with longing of a bone with a little meat on it—how he would enjoy that! So all four got up and made their way toward the light. It grew larger as they came closer. Finally it led them straight to a brightly lighted robbers' den. The donkey, being the tallest, peeped in at the window.

"What do you see, Grayhorse?" whispered the rooster.

"What do I see?" whispered back the donkey in excitement.

"Why, I see a table decked with all manner of delicious food and drink and a band of robbers seated around enjoying every bit of it."

"Ah, that's just what we need," sighed the rooster.

"Yes, but how can we change places?" asked the donkey.

So the four friends talked it over and hit upon a plan to drive the robbers out. The donkey was to place his forefeet upon the window sill, the dog was to jump up on his back, the cat was to climb up on the dog's back, and the rooster was to perch on the cat's head. At a signal, they were all to make their music.

When everything was ready, the signal was given. The donkey brayed, the dog barked, the cat meowed, and the rooster crowed at the top of his lungs. Their music raised such a din that the robbers were terrified, thinking all the devils of the night had been aroused. Then the four musicians burst through the window into the room with such force that they set the windowpanes rattling. The robbers, sure now that every demon in the world was after them, fled helter-skelter into the forest.

The four friends quickly made themselves at home and ate as if they were about to start a month's fast. As soon as they had finished, they put out the light and settled down for the night, each finding the place that suited him best. The donkey made a bed amidst some straw in the yard. The dog chose a spot behind the back door. The cat curled up on the hearth near the warm ashes. And the rooster flew to a perch up in the rafters. They were so tired from their travels that they fell asleep at once.

Shortly after midnight, the robbers noticed that the light had gone out in their den and all seemed quiet. The robber chief said they had all been silly to run away, and he ordered one of the men to go back to the house to see if he could find out what it was that had frightened them out of their wits.

The messenger approached carefully and, finding all still, went into the kitchen to light a candle. Mistaking the cat's glowing eyes for live coals, he held a match close to them to light it. But the cat didn't take to this kind of joke. She sprang at the man, spitting, and scratched his face. Panic-stricken, the robber dropped the match and made for the back door. But the dog, who lay there, leaped up and bit him in the leg. As the frantic robber ran out of the house he crossed the pile of straw in the yard. The donkey lashed out and gave him a good swift kick, while the rooster, awakened by all the noise, called out in his loudest voice: "Cock-a-doodle-do-ee!"

The robber sped like the wind back to his chief. His report was dreadful to hear.

"There's a horrible witch in the house," he gasped when he could speak again. "She flew at me, spitting, and scratched my face with her long sharp claws. By the door stands a man with a knife. He stabbed me as I tried to escape. In the yard lies a dark monster who beat me with a wooden club. And up on the roof sits the judge. He called out, 'Bring the rogue to me.' When I heard this, I took to my heels and nothing in the world will ever make me go back."

None of the robbers dared return to the den after this. But the four travelers were well content with their new home and found it so much to their liking that they did not care to leave it. So, whether they ever went on to Bremen and became town musicians—that is something no one knows.

Snow White and Rose Red

A POOR WIDOW lived with her two daughters in a cottage at the edge of a forest. In front of the cottage stood two rose trees. Each year one bore beautiful white roses, the other, lovely red roses.

The two girls were so like the roses that one was called Snow White, the other Rose Red. Snow White was quiet and gentle; Rose Red was merry and gay. Snow White liked to stay home, helping her mother or reading. Rose Red liked to run about in the fields and meadows, chasing butterflies and picking flowers. Although they were so different, both sisters were good and kind and loved each other dearly.

Often they would go together into the forest to gather berries. They were never afraid, for the wild forest creatures were their friends and never startled or harmed them. Shy rabbits would nibble cabbage

leaves out of their hands; pretty fawns grazed peacefully by their side; and at their approach, birds never flew away, but sang merrily on.

Snow White and Rose Red were good little housekeepers. They kept their mother's cottage so neat and clean that it was a pleasure to enter it. In the summertime, Rose Red dusted and swept every morning. Then she picked a nosegay for her mother, always remembering to put into it a white and a red rose. During the cold winter, it was Snow White who rose early, lit the fire and put the kettle on to boil. The kettle was made of brass but it was so brightly polished that it shone like gold.

When the snow fell in big soft white flakes, mother and daughters liked to sit before the fire. The mother would read out of a big old book stories of kings and princes, witches and fairies, while the girls spun busily and listened spellbound. One evening, when they were sitting thus cosily, there came a knock at the door.

"Quick, Rose Red," said the mother. "Open the door. Perhaps it is a traveler, seeking shelter this bitter cold night."

Rose Red unbolted the door, but instead of a weary traveler there stood in the doorway a big black shaggy bear. Rose Red screamed and Snow White ran and hid behind her mother's bed. Rose Red tried to close the door, but the bear began to speak. "Don't be afraid," he said. "I won't harm any of you. I am cold and tired and only want to warm myself and rest a while."

"Oh, you poor bear," cried the mother. "Come in by all means and warm yourself. But be careful lest a spark from the fire singe your furry coat."

"I'd like the snow brushed off me first," said the bear.

So the mother called Snow White who came out timidly from behind the bed, and to both children she said, "Take your little brooms and brush the snow off the bear. Don't be afraid. He won't hurt you."

This they did and then the bear came into the room. He stretched himself before the fire and grunted in content. He was friendly and gentle and before long the girls were quite at home with him. They came closer and growing bolder began to romp with him and to tease him. They even beat him playfully with a hazel twig. Once when they spanked a little too hard, the bear cried out, "Spare my life, dear children:

Snow White, Rose Red,
Do not beat your wooer dead."

The children had no idea what this meant so they paid little attention. The bear spent the night and in the morning he left. He trotted over the snow into the forest but before night fell he came back. And so throughout the long winter, the bear went out in the morning and returned before dark. The children became so used to him that they left the door unbolted until their shaggy friend had come in.

One morning soon after the snow had melted and Spring had turned the world soft and green again, the bear said to Snow White, "When I leave you today it will be for a long time, for I shall be gone all summer."

"Where must you go then, dear bear?" asked Snow White sadly, for she knew she would miss him.

"I must go into the forest to guard my treasure so that it won't fall into the hands of the wicked dwarfs," the bear told her. "In the winter, when the ground is frozen hard, the dwarfs cannot break through and so my treasure is safe. But now that the sun's warmth has softened the earth, the dwarfs will come out of their holes to steal everything they can."

Snow White was very sad at the thought of not seeing the bear again. She opened the door slowly and the bear, hurrying through, caught his fur on the latch and tore a rent in his coat. It seemed to Snow White that a golden gleam shone through the rent but she could not be sure and she couldn't ask because the bear was already out of sight.

Not long after that the children went into the forest to gather firewood. As they walked about they came to a tree lying across the path, and near its trunk something was jumping up and down in the grass. Curious, the children went up to the trunk to see what it might be. When they came near, they saw a little old wrinkled dwarf with a long white beard the end of which was caught in a crack in the tree.

The little man hopped up and down and pulled and tugged but could not free himself. He glared at the girls and snapped, "Well, are you just going to stand there and not help me?"

"Poor little man, what have you done?" asked Rose Red.

"Done?" snarled the dwarf. "I haven't done anything, you stupid goose. I needed a bit of wood for my fire to cook my simple little meal and was just about to cut into the tree when my hand slipped, the wedge I had put in flew out, and my beautiful white beard got caught in the crack and I cannot get away."

The children tried very hard but they could not free the beard. At last Rose Red said, "I'll go and get some help."

"Oh, you idiots!" sputtered the dwarf in a rage. "You white-faced fools! What good will other mortals do me? There are two too many of you now. Can't you think of something better?"

"Don't be so impatient," said Snow White. "I have thought of something." And she took her scissors out of her pocket and cut off the end of the beard.

The moment he felt himself free the dwarf snatched up a sack of gold that lay between the roots of the tree. He threw it over his shoulder and marched off, grumbling to himself: "Stupid ninnies! The idea! Cutting off my beautiful beard. Bad luck to them!"

A day or so later, Snow White and Rose Red went out to catch a few fish for supper. As they came to the pond, they saw something that looked like a giant grasshopper hopping about on the bank, dangerously close to the water. They ran up and recognized the dwarf.

"You'll fall into the pond if you aren't careful," said Rose Red.

"I'm not such a fool as that," snapped the dwarf. "Don't you see that the fish at the end of my line is trying to pull me in?"

The dwarf had been sitting at the pond's edge, fishing, when a strong wind arose, hopelessly entangling his beard and the fishing line. Just then the dwarf had felt a tug and knew he had caught a fish, but the fish was too big and the little man could not pull him out. Instead it looked as if any moment the fish was going to pull him into the water, unless something happened quickly to help him.

Snow White and Rose Red tried to free the beard from the line but they couldn't do it. So again Snow White took out her scissors and cut off another piece of the long white beard. Instead of being grateful, the dwarf was furious. "You donkey," he stormed. "Are you trying to have me disowned by my people? How can I face them with most of my beautiful white beard gone? You should have worn your feet out before you ran up to me." Snatching up a sack of pearls which lay in the rushes, he dragged it away, muttering and grumbling.

Some time after this Snow White and Rose Red went to town to buy for their mother needles and thread, laces and ribbons. Their way led through a field where great rocks lay strewn about. Overhead they noticed an eagle flying round and round. Slowly it circled and lower it came until suddenly it swooped down behind an enormous rock. At once the children heard a loud frightened cry and running up were horrified to find that the huge bird was carrying off their ill-tempered friend, the dwarf. Snow White seized the little man's coat and Rose Red his beard, and they tugged and pulled so hard that at last the bird gave up the struggle, let go, and flew off.

As soon as he recovered from his fright, the dwarf began to scold as usual. "You clumsy creatures," he ranted. "Couldn't you have been more careful? Look at my coat. It's in shreds. Fools!" He picked up a bag of precious stones and, grumbling all the while, went off to his hole in the ground.

The girls, quite used to the dwarf's bad manners by this time, continued on their way and made their purchases. On the way home, they had to cross the same field. When they came to the place of the big rock, they were surprised to see the dwarf there. He had emptied the sack of gems in a clean spot on the ground, certain that no one would come by at that time of day. The late afternoon sun shone on the gems, making them glow and sparkle with every color of the rainbow. They were so beautiful that Snow White and Rose Red had to stop and admire them.

"What are you gaping at?" shrieked the little man in a frenzy. Before he could say another word, a deep growl was heard and out of the forest came a big black shaggy bear. The terrified dwarf tried to make for his cave but the bear got in his way. Then, very frightened, he whined: "Spare me, dear bear, I am such a skinny little fellow I wouldn't even make an appetizer for you. Spare my life and you shall have my treasure—all this and everything I have hidden in my cave. Take these two wicked girls instead. They're nice and plump and will make a satisfying meal."

The bear paid no attention to the dreadful little man. He gave him one blow with his huge paw and the dwarf did not move again.

By this time Snow White and Rose Red had started to run away, but the bear called after them. "Snow White. Rose Red. Wait for me. I'll not harm you." They knew that voice—it was their old friend of the forest. The girls waited for him and as soon as he came up to them a wonderful thing happened. His shaggy black coat fell off and there before them stood a handsome young prince, clad in shining gold.

"I am a king's son," he told them. "That wicked dwarf had bewitched me and put me under a spell to roam the forest until his death would set me free. Now he has been punished as he richly deserved."

Snow White married him and Rose Red married his brother and they divided between them the treasure that the Prince had hidden from the dwarf. The old mother went to live with her children. She brought with her the two rose trees, and every year they continued to bloom, one with beautiful white roses, the other with lovely red roses.

The Hare and the Hedgehog

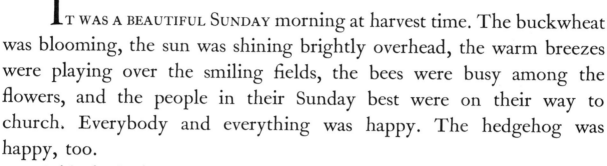

It was a beautiful Sunday morning at harvest time. The buckwheat was blooming, the sun was shining brightly overhead, the warm breezes were playing over the smiling fields, the bees were busy among the flowers, and the people in their Sunday best were on their way to church. Everybody and everything was happy. The hedgehog was happy, too.

This hedgehog was standing in the doorway of his little house, his arms folded on his stomach, enjoying the pleasant Sunday morning. As he stood thus, he hummed a bit of a tune; not a good tune, but not a bad one either. It was no better or worse, in fact, than the tunes all hedgehogs were accustomed to hum on a perfect Sunday morning.

In the midst of his humming, it suddenly occurred to the hedgehog that, while his wife was washing and dressing the children, he might take a walk to see how his turnips were getting along. The hedgehog called them "his turnips" but they were his only because they grew in the field next to his house. As the hedgehog and his family often helped themselves to the turnips, they had quite naturally begun to regard the turnip patch as theirs.

From thinking to doing was the work of a moment. The hedgehog closed the door and went down the road to the turnip field. He had not gone far when he came upon his neighbor, the hare, doing exactly the same thing, except that the hare's interest was in cabbages, not in turnips. The hedgehog, a good-natured fellow, gave the hare

a cheery "Good-morning." But the hare fancied himself a gentleman of importance. He looked at the hedgehog haughtily and did not return the friendly greeting. Instead, he said scornfully, "What brings you out in the field so early in the morning?"

"I am taking a walk," said the hedgehog.

"A walk!" sneered the hare. "Can't you put your legs to better use?"

Now this made the hedgehog very angry. His crooked legs had been given him by nature, it is true; nevertheless he did not like anyone to mention them or to make remarks about them. So he said to the hare:

"Do you think you can do more with your legs than I can with mine?"

"I certainly do," said the hare proudly.

"That can easily be proved," said the hedgehog. "I'm sure if we were to run a race, I would be the winner."

The hare thought this was ridiculous. The hedgehog should be taught a lesson for even daring to suggest such a thing! So he agreed to race against him.

"What shall we wager?" he asked.

"A gold piece and a bottle of wine," said the hedgehog.

"Done!" cried the hare. "Let's start at once."

"Oh, there's no hurry," said the hedgehog. "I haven't had my breakfast yet. Suppose I go home first, have a bite to eat, and meet you in half an hour?"

The hare didn't mind, so the hedgehog hurried home. On the way, he wondered how he might outwit the hare. "He's long on legs," he thought, "but short on brains. He thinks he's a great fellow but he's really a ninny, and I'll make him pay for his insults."

When he reached home, the hedgehog said to his wife, "Hurry. Drop everything and come with me."

"What are you up to now?" asked his wife.

"I have wagered the hare a gold piece and a bottle of wine that I will beat him in a race," the hedgehog told her.

"Mercy on us!" exclaimed his wife. "Have you taken leave of your senses? How can you possibly win against the hare with his long, swift legs?"

"Woman," cried the hedgehog, "don't try to understand the

affairs of men! This business doesn't concern you. Just do as I say."

So what could the wife do but obey? Without another word, she went out with her husband. On the way to the field, the hedgehog said, "Listen carefully to what I am going to tell you. I'll suggest to the hare that we run our race in the long field. He will run in one furrow and I in the other. Now, I want you to stay quietly at the bottom of my furrow and when the hare arrives at that end you must get up and cry out, 'Here I am already.'"

When they got to the field, the hedgehog showed his wife her place, and then he joined the hare.

"Are you ready?" asked the hare.

"Ready," said the hedgehog.

"Then," said the hare, "one, two, three—and off we go!"

Like a flash of lightning, the hare streaked off. The hedgehog ran a few paces, crouched low in his furrow, and remained there. When the hare, puffing like a locomotive, arrived at the end of the furrow, the hedgehog's wife popped up in the other furrow and exclaimed:

"Here I am already!"

The hare couldn't believe his eyes and his ears, for of course as the hedgehog's wife looked exactly like her husband, he had no doubt but that it was the hedgehog who stood there talking to him. He couldn't understand how it had happened.

"There must be some mistake," he thought, and aloud he said:

"A return match. We must have a return match. Let's run again."

The hedgehog was willing. Once again, the hare went off like the wind, but the hedgehog's wife remained quietly in her place. When the hare reached the top of the furrow, the hedgehog himself jumped up and called out: "Here I am already."

"It's not fair. It's not fair," raged the hare. "Let's try it again."

"As often as you wish," the hedgehog replied. So the hare raced

again and again, and each time when he reached the top or the bottom of the furrow, the hedgehog was always there ahead of him. In all, the hare ran against the hedgehog seventy-three times, but at the seventy-fourth time, his strength gave out. He couldn't even finish this last run but dropped down exhausted in the middle of the furrow.

The hedgehog collected the gold piece, the bottle of wine, and his wife, and went home. No doubt he is still living there beside the turnip patch in great content. And since that time no hare has ever run a race against a hedgehog.

This story, like all good stories, has a moral; in fact, two morals. The first is, never make fun of anyone about a condition he cannot help. And the second is, when you marry, be careful to marry someone just like yourself. Especially if you are a hedgehog, you should make doubly sure that you marry no one but another hedgehog.

The Shoemaker and the Elves

THERE WAS ONCE a poor shoemaker who was as unlucky as he was honest. For the harder he worked the poorer he became. At last a day arrived when he had nothing left but just enough leather for one pair of shoes. Nevertheless, he cut the leather out carefully, placed the pieces on his work table, and planned to get up early in the morning to sew the shoes. Then the good man said his prayers and went peacefully to bed.

Imagine his surprise next morning when he found on the table a finished pair of shoes. And such shoes! The astonished man turned them this way and that, examining them from every side, but could find no fault. They were so beautifully made and so perfectly sewn that it was clear a craftsman had fashioned them. With a silent prayer of thanks, the shoemaker put the shoes in his shop window. Soon a customer came. He appreciated the fine workmanship and because he

was so pleased with the shoes, he paid more than the usual price.

With the money the shoemaker was able to buy leather for two more pairs. Again he cut the leather out carefully and placed the pieces on his work table. And again the next morning he found that the pieces had been turned into two pairs of pretty shoes. Once more the shoemaker sold them for a good price and bought enough leather this time for four pairs of shoes. That night, as before, he prepared the leather and the following morning the same sight met his eyes: four pairs of shoes with not so much as one false or uneven stitch in the lot.

And so it went. The shoemaker continued to buy leather which he cut out every night, and each morning he awoke to find the shoes finished. They were always so beautiful that the shoemaker got better and better prices for them. Soon he was poor no longer.

One night, just before Christmas, the shoemaker said to his wife: "Wife, would you not like to know who or what it is that has been so good to us? What do you say we keep watch this night?"

The wife agreed, and so, after cutting out the leather as usual, the shoemaker and his wife hid in a corner of the room behind some clothes hanging there. Just as the clock struck twelve, two naked little elves pranced in. They sped to the table and went to work. All night long their nimble fingers flew, stitching, sewing, hammering, until all the pieces of leather had been turned into shoes fit for royalty. Then they disappeared.

The next day, the shoemaker's wife said, "Husband, I've been thinking. The elves have made us rich. Should we not let them know how grateful we are? They must be cold, poor little tykes, running about without a stitch on. I'd like to make a tiny suit for each of them and knit them each a pair of warm stockings. And how would you like to make them each a pair of shoes?"

"I'd like that very much," said the shoemaker, and he gladly sat down to work. The little shirts and vests, coats and trousers, shoes and stockings were soon ready. One night, instead of the usual pieces of leather, the shoemaker placed the gay presents on his work table. Then he and his wife hid again behind the clothes in the corner to see what the elves would do. Just as the clock struck twelve, they pranced in. At first, when they didn't find any leather, they were surprised. But as they picked up each piece of clothing and realized it was meant for them, they were delighted. They dressed themselves in a flash. Then they began to skip and dance merrily around the room. Leaping over chairs and benches, they gaily sang:

> *Now that well-dressed lads are we,*
> *No longer need we cobblers be.*

At last they danced out of the room and out of sight. They never came back. But the good luck they had brought the shoemaker stayed with him. From that time on, his labor was always rewarded, and he continued to prosper until the end of his days.

Rumpelstiltskin

THERE WAS ONCE A POOR MILLER who had a very beautiful daughter. It happened that the miller had to call on the King and, as he wished to appear important, he said, "It may interest your Majesty to know that my daughter can spin straw into gold."

"Such a trick interests me indeed," said the King. "If your daughter is as clever as you say, bring her to the palace tomorrow and we shall soon find out."

So the miller's daughter was brought to the palace and placed in a room full of straw. A spinning wheel and bobbins were brought.

"Now let us see if you are as clever as your father says," the King told her. "I want all this straw spun into gold before morning or you will lose your life."

And he himself locked the door securely, and left.

The poor girl sat there, staring at all the straw, the spinning wheel and the bobbins. Not for the life of her did she know what to do. As the hours went by, she grew more and more frightened and at last burst into tears. Suddenly the door opened and a crooked little man appeared.

"Miller's daughter," said he, "why do you weep?"

"Alas," sobbed the girl, "unless all this straw is spun into gold before morning I shall die."

"What will you give me," asked the little man, "if I help you?"

"My necklace," said the girl.

The little man took her necklace and sat down at the spinning wheel. *Whirr. Whirr. Whirr.* In no more than three times around the bobbin was full of gold. Then he took another bobbin, and *whirr, whirr, whirr!* Three times around, and it too was full. And so on throughout the night until he had spun all the straw into glistening gold.

When the King arrived early in the morning and saw the gold, he was delighted. But he also became more greedy. So he had the girl placed in a larger room filled with straw. Again he told her if she valued her life to see to it that all the straw was spun into gold before morning.

Poor girl. What could she do? She had no more idea now than before how to spin gold from straw. As she began to cry, the door opened and there stood the little man. He did not have to be told why she was crying.

"What will you give me," he asked, "if I help you again?"

"My ring," said the girl, and she took it off her finger. The little man snatched the ring, seated himself at the spinning wheel, and went to work. Before the night was over, all the straw had been spun into shining gold.

The King was very pleased. But the more gold he had, the more he wanted. So he brought the miller's daughter to the largest room in the palace. It was *stuffed* with straw, from floor to ceiling.

"If you spin all this into gold before morning," he said, "I will marry you and you will be Queen. But if you do not, you shall lose your life." To himself he thought, "True, she is only a miller's daughter, but she is very pretty, and where will I find anyone more gifted or clever?"

No sooner did the King leave the girl when the little man appeared.

"What will you give me," he asked, "if I help you now?"

"I have nothing more to give you," said the girl, sadly.

"Then promise me your first child after you become Queen," said he.

The miller's daughter looked around at the room stuffed with straw and thought not even the little man could help her this time. "Then who knows whether I shall ever be Queen," she said to herself. And so she promised.

But the little man did spin all the straw into gleaming gold, and before morning, too! When the King saw this, he kept his word, and the miller's daughter became Queen after all.

A year later, a beautiful baby was born to her. The Queen had forgotten all about the crooked little man. One day, as she was playing with her baby, he suddenly appeared and demanded that she keep her promise. She offered him every treasure in the kingdom instead of the child, but the little man said he preferred a living thing to all the riches in the world. The Queen wept and begged and pleaded and at last he took pity on her.

"I will give you three days. If you guess my name within that time, you may keep the child," he said.

All night the Queen stayed awake, trying to recall every name she had ever heard. She also sent a messenger around the kingdom to see what others he might discover.

When the little man appeared on the first day, she said: "Is your name Caspar?"

"No."

"Is your name Melchior?"

"No."

"Is your name Balthazar?"

"No."

And no matter what name she mentioned, he always said, "No. That is not my name."

The second day she thought she would try unusual names. So she said:

"Is your name Bandylegs?"

"No."

"Is your name Crooked Back?"

"No."

"Is your name Long-nose?"

"No."

And no matter what unusual name she mentioned, he always said, "No. That is not my name."

As the third day drew near, the poor Queen thought and thought, but not another name that she had not already mentioned could she recall. As she sat thus, her messenger returned.

"I haven't been able to find a single strange name," he reported, "but I did see something funny today. As I was riding through the forest, I saw off in the distance a crooked little man. He was dancing around an open fire and as he danced, he sang:

> "*Today I brew, tomorrow bake,*
> *The next the young Queen's child I'll take.*
> *How good that neither man nor dame*
> *Knows Rumpelstiltskin is my name.*"

Well! Can you imagine how happy the Queen was to hear this? But when the little man appeared on the third day, she pretended to be very worried.

"Is your name Tom?" she asked anxiously.

"No."

"Is your name Dick?"

"No," he said, and reached for the child.

"There is only one other name I know," said the Queen, holding the child closer. "Perhaps it is yours." She looked down at the little man and said:

"Is your name Rumpelstiltskin?"

"The devil told you that! The devil told you that!" he cried in a rage, and stamped his foot so hard that he sank into the ground. And that was the end of him.

The Golden Goose

THERE WAS A MAN who had three sons, the youngest of whom was called Simpleton. The others teased and mocked him all the time.

One day the eldest son decided to go to the forest to cut wood. His mother fixed him a nice lunch of a cake made with eggs and a bottle of wine. No sooner had he entered the forest when he met a little old gray-haired man who gave him a kind "Good-morning" and then said, "Please give me a bite of your cake and a sip of your wine, for I am hungry and thirsty."

But the clever son said, "If I give you a bite of cake and a sip of wine, I'll have that much less for myself. So be off with you, old man!"

And leaving the old man standing there, the eldest son went about his business. However, when he began to hew down the tree, the ax slipped and cut his arm. So he had to stop working and go home to have it bound up. Now this was no accident; oh no; it was the doing of the little old gray-haired man.

Then the second son said he would go to the forest to cut wood. For him too the mother put up a nice lunch of a cake made with eggs and a bottle of wine. Just like the first, the second son met the little old gray-haired man who asked him for a bite of his cake and a sip of his wine.

But this one spoke as cleverly as his brother: "Whatever I give you," he said, "will mean that much less for myself. So be off with you, old man!" And he too left the old man standing there while he went

into the forest. You may be sure his punishment was not long delayed. No sooner had he lifted his ax to strike the tree when his arm slipped, the ax came down on his leg and cut so deep a gash he had to be carried home.

Then Simpleton said: "Father, let me go into the forest to cut wood for you."

But the father replied: "Your brothers, who are so much wiser, were not able to do anything but get hurt. You know nothing about it. Better let well enough alone."

But Simpleton begged so hard that at last his father sighed and said: "Go then, if you must. You'll know better when you've hurt yourself."

For his lunch, the mother gave him a cake made only with water and baked in the ashes and with it a bottle of sour beer. When he entered the forest, like his brothers Simpleton met the little old gray-haired man who said, "I am so hungry and thirsty. Won't you give me a bite of your cake and a sip of your wine?"

"It's but a cinder cake," said Simpleton. "And in this bottle is no wine; only sour beer. However, if such food is to your liking, I'll gladly share it with you."

So they sat down and when the boy took out his cake, he found it had turned into a nice sweet one, and when he poured the sour beer, good red wine came out of the bottle. So they ate and drank together and when they were done, the little old gray-haired man said, "Because you have a kind heart and are willing to share what is yours with others, I will give you good luck. Do you see that old tree? Cut it down and you will find something at the roots." Then he disappeared.

Simpleton lost no time. He went up to the old tree and with a few sure strokes soon had it cut down. And what do you think he found sitting amidst the gnarled roots? A goose. But not just any

goose. This one had feathers of pure gold! Simpleton picked her up and took her with him to an inn where he planned to spend the night.

The innkeeper had three sharp-eyed daughters who noticed the wonderful bird at once. They longed for one of the golden feathers, and the eldest daughter kept an eye out for a chance to get one. As soon as Simpleton stepped out of the room, she ran up to the goose and took hold of its wing, meaning to pluck out a feather. But to her dismay, she found her fingers and hand stuck fast to the goose, and she could not pull herself away.

The second daughter then came over with the same idea in mind, but barely had she touched her sister when she too was stuck fast. The third, when she saw the two together, thought she should join them. But when she came over, the other two cried out, "Stay away. Don't touch us!" The youngest daughter did not understand this. "Why should I stay away?" she asked. "I want to be with you." So saying, she touched the middle sister and, like the others, remained stuck fast. And so the three had to pass the night held fast to the golden goose.

The next morning, Simpleton took the goose under his arm, paying no attention to the three girls hanging on behind. They had a dreadful time, poor things, running now on the right, now on the left, in order to keep from tripping over Simpleton's legs.

In this manner they went along until they came to the center of the town where they met the parson. "Aren't you ashamed, you bold girls?" cried out the good man. "Do you think it is proper to run after a young man like this?"

He reached out for the hand of the youngest sister, intending to pull her away, but no sooner did he touch her when he found himself held fast. And try as he would he could not pry loose. So, willy nilly, he too joined the parade.

They had not gone far when the sexton came along. Astounded to see the parson running after three young women, he called, "Stop, your reverence! Where are you going so fast? Have you forgotten there is a christening this afternoon?" And catching up with the group, he took hold of the parson's sleeve. No sooner had the sexton done so when he found himself unable to let go.

By and by two field workers carrying their hoes came along, and the parson called out to them to set free the sexton and himself. But as soon as they touched them, the laborers found they were held fast like all the rest. So now there were seven in the parade, one treading on the heels of the other, as they all followed Simpleton and the golden goose.

In this fashion they traveled on until they came to a city. Now, the King who ruled this city had an only daughter who was so solemn no one had ever been able to make her laugh. So the King had decreed that whoever could make his daughter laugh could have her for his wife.

When Simpleton heard this he marched up to the palace, right in front of the Princess's window. The Princess took one look at the silly parade—the three daughters of the innkeeper, the parson, the sexton and the two field workers, all stuck fast to each other, all weaving and stumbling after Simpleton and his goose; and she burst into such loud gales of laughter it seemed she would never stop. So Simpleton went to the King and asked for the Princess in marriage.

But the King did not fancy a simple fellow for a son-in-law, so he said he would consent only under certain conditions. First, he said, Simpleton must find someone who could drink a cellar full of wine.

"Only one person can help me," thought Simpleton, "the little old gray-haired man." Back to the forest he hurried, and on the same spot where he had cut down the tree he found a man with a sad face.

"What is your trouble?" asked Simpleton.

"Alas," said the man, "I have such a powerful thirst nothing seems to quench it. Cold water I hate, and I have just finished a huge cask of wine; but for a thirst like mine that was no more than a drop on a burning stone."

"Your troubles are over, my friend," said Simpleton. "Come with me and even your thirst will soon be satisfied." He took him to the King's cellar. The man started in at once on the casks of wine and by the end of the day not a drop was left in any of them.

Then Simpleton once more asked the King to give him the Princess for his wife. But the King couldn't bear the thought of having his only daughter marry anyone called Simpleton. So he made a new condition. Now the boy was to find someone who could eat a mountain of bread. Simpleton did not think long. Straight to the forest he went, and in the same spot as before, he found a man pulling his belt tightly around his body and making the most terrible faces.

"What's the matter?" asked Simpleton. "You look near death."

"Quite so," said the man. "The only way I can stay alive is to keep my belt tight around me. I have such an awful appetite I am always hungry. I've just eaten an ovenful of rolls but my stomach is still empty."

"Follow me," said Simpleton happily, "and I promise that your appetite will soon be satisfied." He led the man to the palace where all the flour in the kingdom had been collected and baked into a mountain of bread. The man sat down before it and by nightfall the mountain was gone. Then Simpleton again demanded the Princess for his wife. But the King tried once more to get rid of him. He ordered him to find a ship that could sail on both land and sea. "And when you come sailing in that," he said, "you shall have the Princess."

Simpleton headed straight for the forest. This time he found the little old gray-haired man himself—the one with whom he had shared his cinder cake and his sour beer. The man said, "I have eaten and drunk for you, and I shall give you the ship, too. All this I do for you because you have a good heart and you were kind to me."

Then he gave Simpleton the ship that could sail on both land and sea, and when the King saw this he could no longer refuse him the Princess, his daughter. So the wedding took place at once, and when the old King died, Simpleton inherited the kingdom. He ruled wisely, and lived happily many long years with his Princess.

The Sleeping Beauty

ONCE UPON A TIME there were a King and a Queen who made a wish every day. It was always the same wish. "Oh, if we could only have a child," they sighed.

One day, as the Queen was bathing, a frog crawled out of the water, plopped down on the land, and said to her, "Your wish will come true. Before the year passes, you will have a little daughter."

And it happened just as the frog said. Before the year was over, the Queen had a child, a little girl so lovely that the King's joy knew no bounds.

He ordered a great feast to celebrate the child's birth, and to it he invited all his relatives, his friends, and his neighbors. And so that the little princess might have the best of godmothers, he also invited the Wise Women. There were thirteen in the kingdom, but as the King had only twelve golden plates for them to eat off, the invitations were sent to twelve, and one of the Wise Women had to stay at home.

The feast was celebrated with all splendor. As it drew to an end, the Wise Women stepped forward to bestow upon the baby their wonderful gifts. One gave her virtue, another beauty, a third wealth, and so on until eleven had spoken. Everything good in the world that one could wish for was given the princess. Just as the eleventh Wise Woman finished talking, suddenly there rushed into the hall the thirteenth—the one who had had to stay at home. Furious at not having been invited and thinking only of revenge, she cried out:

"In her fifteenth year the Princess shall prick herself with a spindle and fall down dead!"

The shocked guests were horror-stricken but no one knew what to do. However, the twelfth Wise Woman who had not yet bestowed her gift, now said gently, "I cannot take away this evil curse, but at least I can soften it. When the Princess falls down, it will not be in death, but in a deep sleep from which she shall awake when a hundred years have gone by."

The King wanted to spare his beloved child even this dreadful fate, so he ordered every spindle in the kingdom to be burned.

As time went by, the wishes of the Wise Women were fulfilled. Never had there been a princess so beautiful and clever and so modest and good, too. Whoever saw her loved her at once. And so one year followed another until the day of the Princess' fifteenth birthday arrived.

It happened that on this very day the King and the Queen were unable to be home. Left to herself, the Princess decided to explore the castle. She went from room to room, peeking into one chamber, visiting in another, until at last she came to an old forgotten tower in an unused part of the castle. A narrow winding staircase led up to a door. The Princess could see a rusty key in the lock. Curious, she climbed up the stairs and turned the key. The door flew open and there in a little room sat an old, old woman, spindle in hand, busily spinning flax.

"Good day to you, little old granny," said the Princess. "What are you doing?"

"I am spinning, child," said the old woman, nodding her head.

"Spinning?" said the Princess. "What is spinning, and what is that thing you are holding that whirls around so gaily?" And she put out her hand for the spindle, thinking that she would like to try to spin. But no sooner did she touch the spindle than the curse of the thirteenth Wise Woman took effect. She pricked her finger, fell down upon the bed which stood there, and went into a deep, deep sleep.

In that instant the curse also fell upon the whole castle. The King and the Queen who had just returned and were in the Throne Room fell asleep, and the whole court with them. In the stable the horses went to sleep; in the yard, the dogs. The pigeons on the roof and the flies on the walls went to sleep. The fire that had been leaping and crackling on the hearth died down, the spit stopped turning, and the huge roast sizzled no more.

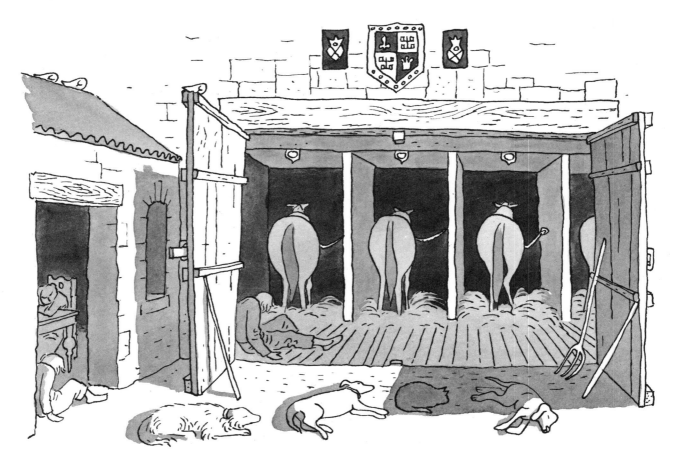

The cook who was just about to pull the scullery boy's hair for something he had forgotten to do, let him go and they both went to sleep, while the little kitchen maid stopped plucking the black hen in her lap and fell asleep, still holding on to the fowl. Outside the wind stopped blowing and not a leaf stirred on any of the trees. All around the castle a hedge of thorns sprang up. Every year it grew higher and higher, hiding the castle until finally nothing could be seen of it, not even the banner that no longer fluttered on the roof.

As time went on a legend grew up in that country about the castle behind the hedge of thorns. People whispered among themselves and passed on to their children and grandchildren the story of the Princess Briar Rose, for so the King's daughter had been named, who slept behind the hedge in the castle with her parents, the King and the Queen, and all the court. They said she was clever and kind and more beautiful than words could tell, and hearing this story many a King's son tried to rescue her. But although the princes were all brave and daring not one could get through the hedge of thorns.

Long, long years passed and at last there came a prince who listened in wonder as an old man told him the story of Briar Rose, the sleeping beauty.

"I am determined to save her," cried the Prince, but the old man tried to discourage him. He told him of the many princes who had already tried only to fall victim to the cruel thorns.

"I am not afraid," said the Prince. "I will rescue the beautiful Briar Rose," and he set off at once for the hidden castle.

Now, was it not wonderful that unknown to the Prince the last day of the hundred years had arrived? When the Prince reached the thorn hedge, it burst into bloom. The lovely flowers parted of their own accord, made a path for him, and let him pass unharmed. Then they closed again behind him and turned into a hedge once more.

The young Prince walked about, astonished at all he saw. In the

yard lay the dogs, fast asleep; in the stables, the horses. On the roof
sat the pigeons with their heads tucked under their wings. When the
Prince entered the castle, he saw the flies sleeping on the walls, and in
the great hall, the King and the Queen sleeping beside their thrones.
In the kitchen slept the cook, her hand still reaching for the scullery
boy's hair, and the little kitchen maid still sat there with the black hen
in her lap.

From room to room went the Prince, marveling. It was so quiet
that he could hear his own breath come and go. At last he reached
the tower and the narrow winding staircase that led to the little chamber
where Briar Rose lay asleep. The Prince turned the rusty key, the
door sprang open, and then he saw her — a Princess so enchanting that
he could not take his eyes away. He leaned over and kissed her. Briar
Rose opened her eyes and gave him a lovely, happy smile.

Then together they went downstairs and at once the King and
the Queen and the whole court awoke and rubbed their eyes and
looked at each other in great surprise.

All through the castle everyone and everything began to stir and to pick up where they had left off a hundred years before. The horses in the stable awoke and shook their manes. The dogs jumped up in the courtyard, barked and wagged their tails. The pigeons began to coo and spread their wings. The flies started to walk on the walls. On the hearth, the fire leaped up and began to crackle, the spit started to turn and the roast to sizzle. The cook at last gave the scullery boy's hair so sharp a yank that he yelled out loud, and the little kitchen maid finished plucking the black hen.

As for Briar Rose and her Prince, their wedding was celebrated soon after much joy and merriment, and they lived happily all the rest of their days.

RANDOM HOUSE BOOKS FOR CHILDREN

Question and Answer Books

For ages 6-10:
Question and Answer Book of Nature
Question and Answer Book of Science
Question and Answer Book of Space
Question and Answer Book About the
  Human Body

Gateway Books

For ages 8 and up:
The Friendly Dolphins
The Horse that Swam Away
Champ: Gallant Collie
Mystery of the Musical Umbrella
and other titles

Step-Up Books

For ages 7-8:
Animals Do the Strangest Things
Birds Do the Strangest Things
Fish Do the Strangest Things
Meet Abraham Lincoln
Meet John F. Kennedy
and other titles

Babar Books

For ages 4 and up:
The Story of Babar
Babar the King
The Travels of Babar
Babar Comes to America
and other titles

Books by Dr. Seuss

For ages 5 and up:
Dr. Seuss's Sleep Book
Happy Birthday to You!
Horton Hatches the Egg
Horton Hears a Who
If I Ran the Zoo
I Had Trouble in Getting to Solla
  Sollew
McElligot's Pool
On Beyond Zebra
Scrambled Eggs Super!
The Sneetches
Thidwick: The Big-Hearted Moose
Yertle the Turtle
and other titles

Giant Picture Books

For ages 5 and up:
Abraham Lincoln
Big Black Horse
Big Book of Things to Do and
  Make
Big Book of Tricks and Magic
Blue Fairy Book
Daniel Boone
Famous Indian Tribes
George Washington
Hiawatha
King Arthur
Peter Pan
Robert E. Lee
Robin Hood
Robinson Crusoe
Three Little Horses
Three Little Horses at the King's
  Palace

Beginner Books

For ages 5-7:
The Cat in the Hat Beginner Book
  Dictionary
The Cat in the Hat
The Cat in the Hat Comes Back
Dr. Seuss's ABC Book
Green Eggs and Ham
Go, Dog, Go!
Bennett Cerf's Book of Riddles
The King, the Mice and the Cheese
and other titles

Picture Books

For ages 4 and up:
Poems to Read to the Very Young
Songs to Sing with the Very Young
Stories to Read to the Very Young
Alice in Wonderland
Anderson's Fairy Tales
Bambi's Children
Black Beauty
Favorite Tales for the Very Young
Grandmas and Grandpas
Grimm's Fairy Tales
Heidi
Little Lost Kitten
Mother Goose
Once-Upon-A-Time Storybook
Pinocchio
Puppy Dog Tales
Read-Aloud Nursery Tales
Sleeping Beauty
The Sleepytime Storybook
Stories that Never Grow Old
The Wild and Wooly Animal Book
The Wizard of Oz

RANDOM HOUSE, INC., NEW YORK, N. Y.

Grimm's Fairy Tales

The Hare and

The Shoemaker and the Elves

The Sleeping Beauty

The Brave Little Tailor